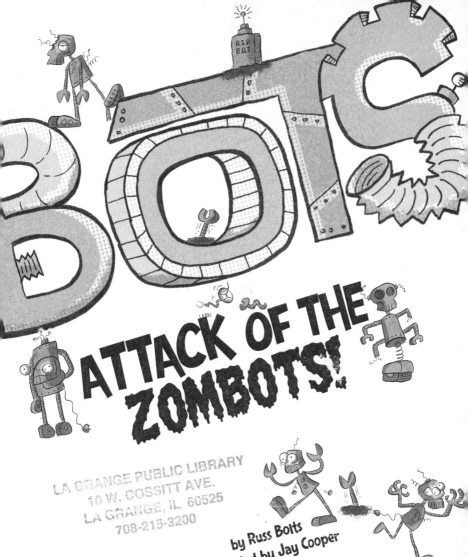

BOTS

ATTACK OF THE ZOMBOTS!

by Russ Bolts
illustrated by Jay Cooper

LITTLE SIMON

New York   London   Toronto   Sydney   New Delhi

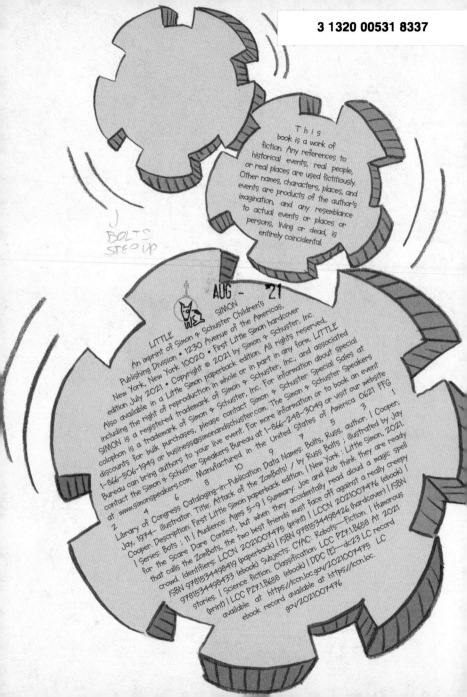

3 1320 00531 8337

J
BOLTS
STEP UP

AUG – '21

LITTLE SIMON
An imprint of Simon & Schuster Children's
Publishing Division • 1230 Avenue of the Americas,
New York, New York 10020 • First Little Simon hardcover
edition July 2021 • Copyright © 2021 by Simon & Schuster, Inc.
Also available in a Little Simon paperback edition. All rights reserved,
including the right of reproduction in whole or in part in any form. LITTLE
SIMON is a registered trademark of Simon & Schuster, Inc., and associated
colophon is a trademark of Simon & Schuster, Inc. For information about special
discounts for bulk purchases, please contact Simon & Schuster Special Sales at
1-866-506-1949 or business@simonandschuster.com. The Simon & Schuster Speakers
Bureau can bring authors to your live event. For more information or to book an event
contact the Simon & Schuster Speakers Bureau at 1-866-248-3049 or visit our website
at www.simonspeakers.com. Manufactured in the United States of America 0621 FFG
2   4   6   8   10   9   7   5   3   1
Library of Congress Cataloging-in-Publication Data Names: Bolts, Russ, author. | Cooper,
Jay, 1974– illustrator. Title: Attack of the ZomBots! / by Russ Bolts ; illustrated by Jay
Cooper. Description: First Little Simon paperback edition. | New York : Little Simon, 2021. |
Series: Bots ; 11 | Audience: Ages 5–9 | Summary: Joe and Rob think they are ready
for the Scare Dare Contest, but when they accidentally read aloud a really creepy
that calls the ZomBots, the two best friends must face off against a magic spell
crowd. Identifiers: LCCN 2021007475 (print) | LCCN 2021007476 (ebook) | ISBN
9781534498419 (paperback) | ISBN 9781534498426 (hardcover) | ISBN
9781534498433 (ebook) Subjects: CYAC: Robots—Fiction. | Humorous
stories. | Science fiction. Classification: LCC PZ7.1.B658 At 2021
(print) | LCC PZ7.1.B658 (ebook) | DDC [E]—dc23 LC record
available at https://lccn.loc.gov/2021007475 LC
ebook record available at https://lccn.loc.
gov/2021007476

CONTENTS

CHAPTER 1

Bright and Early

Ah, good morning, Bot fans! It looks like a peaceful day in Botsburg.

Yep, nothing could go wrong on a day like this. See? Joe Bot is fast asleep in his room.

Here comes his mother to wake him up.

WRESTLE BOT!

3

4

5

8

11

CLICK!

16

CHAPTER 2

Scare Dare Day

Dear friends, if this is your first Scare Dare Day, then raise your hand.

Now put it down because I cannot see you.

I am only the narrator in this book, silly.

19

Scare Dare Day is when Bots play pranks on each other.

The bigger the scare, the bigger the scream... and the bigger the scream, the bigger the fun.

21

Most Bots *love* Scare Dare Day.

But not Joe.

WOOOO!

Oh, he's been scared before...

...but never on Scare Dare Day.

YAWN

BLAH! BLAH!

30

31

34

37

41

42

43

CHAPTER 4
ZOMBOTS
Back in town, things were very quiet. *Too* quiet.
Hmm, it's quiet.
Too quiet. Keep your head up. This feels like a Scare Dare Day trap.
RUN!
AAH!

51

Hmm, Joe and Rob are busy worrying about Squish.
But who is busy worrying about Joe and Rob?
Because the ZomBots have come to town.
And they look hungry.

53

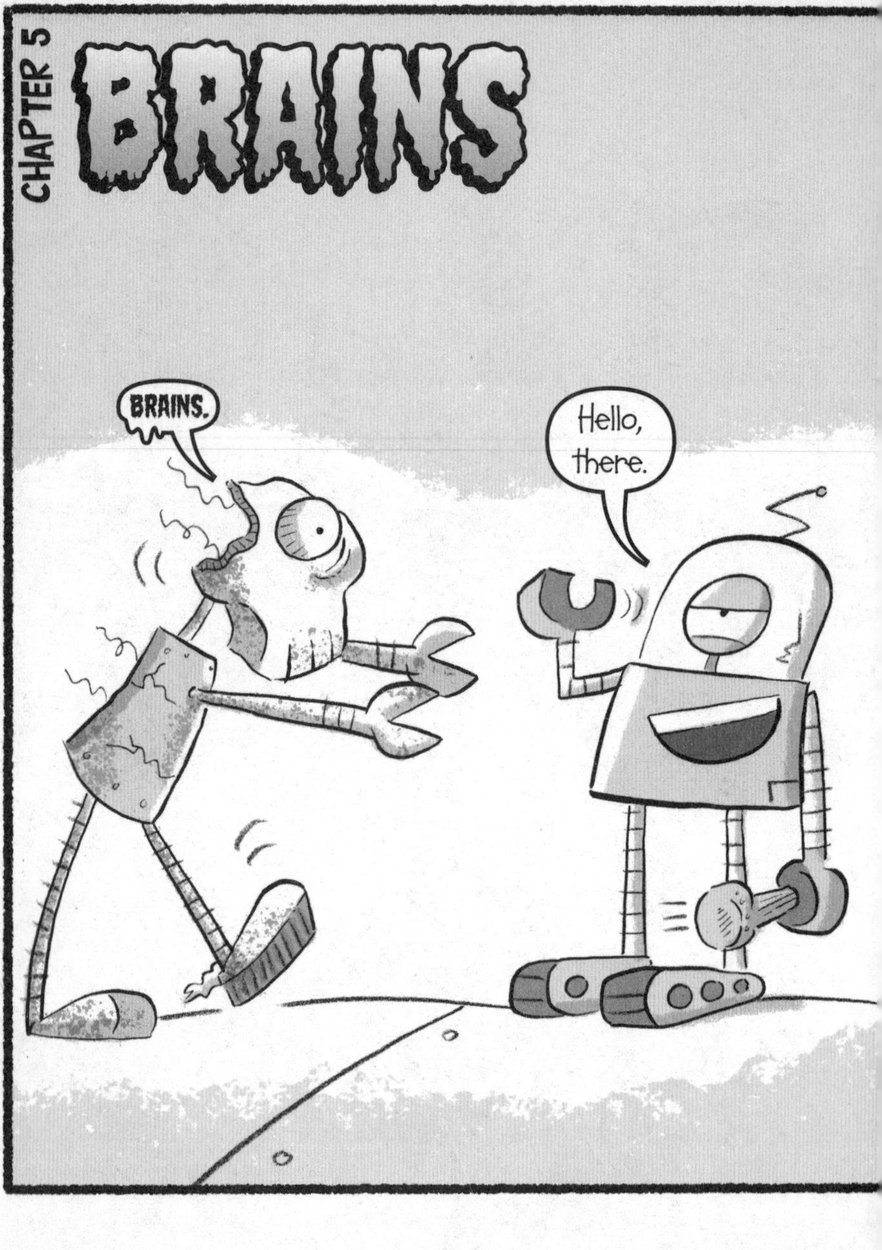
CHAPTER 5
BRAINS
BRAINS.
Hello, there.

59

62

64

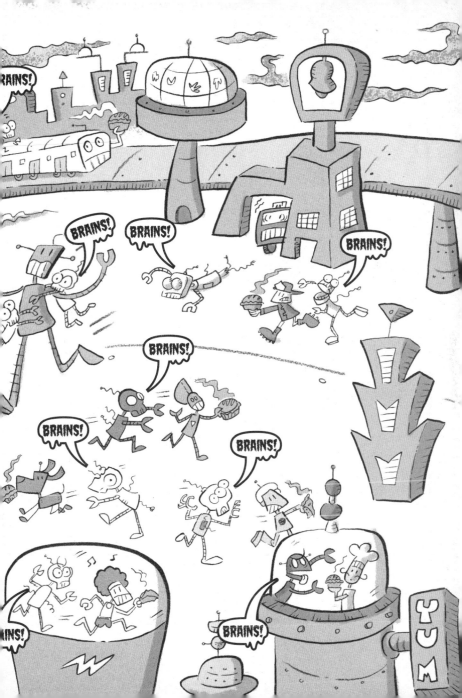

81

84

89

91

93

CHAPTER 8 Mom-ster

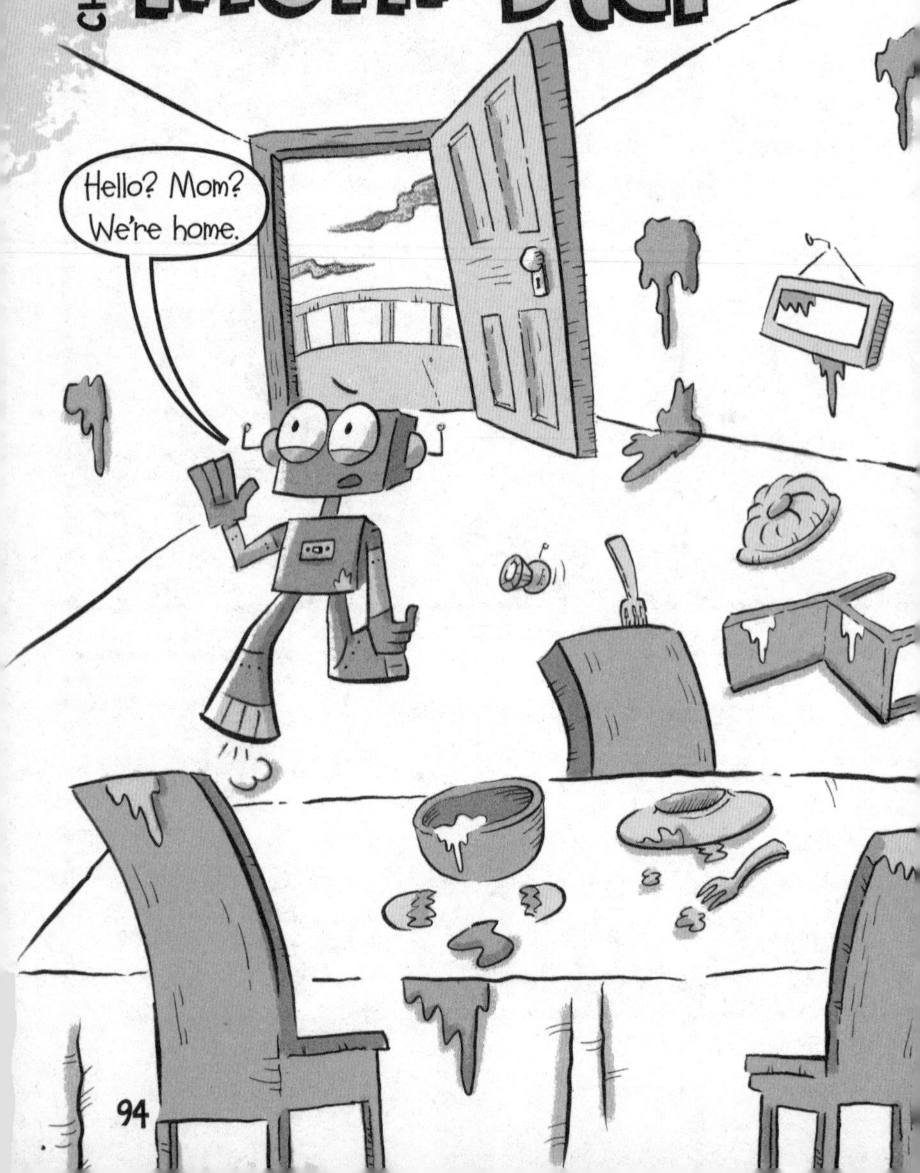

95

96

99

101

107

108

113

Made You Scream